Selected from

THE
WOMEN OF
BREWSTER
PLACE

Gloria Naylor

WRITERS' VOICES
SIGNAL HILL

ATTENTION READERS: We would like to hear what you think about our books. Please send your comments or suggestions to:

Signal Hill Publications
P.O. Box 131
Syracuse, NY 13210-0131

Selection: From THE WOMEN OF BREWSTER PLACE by Gloria Naylor. © 1981 by Gloria Naylor. Reprinted by permission of Sterling Lord Literistic, Inc. and Viking Penguin, a division of Penguin USA.

SIGNAL HILL

Additional material
© 1991 Signal Hill Publications
A publishing imprint of Laubach Literacy International

10 9 8 7 6 5 4 3 2

First printing: March 1991

ISBN 0-929631-33-1

The words 'Writers' Voices' are a trademark of Signal Hill Publications.

Cover designed by Paul Davis Studio
Interior designed by Caron Harris

Signal Hill is a not-for-profit publisher. The proceeds from the sale of this book go to support the national and international programs of Laubach Literacy International.

PRINTED WITH
SOY INK

This book was printed on 100% recycled paper which contains 50% post-consumer waste.

Acknowledgments

We gratefully acknowledge the generous support of the following foundations and corporations that made the publication of WRITERS' VOICES and NEW WRITERS' VOICES possible: An anonymous foundation; The Vincent Astor Foundation; Booth Ferris Foundation; Exxon Corporation; James Money Management, Inc.; Knight Foundation; Philip Morris Companies Inc.; Scripps Howard Foundation; The House of Seagram; and H.W. Wilson Foundation.

This book could not have been realized without the kind and generous cooperation of the author, Gloria Naylor, her publisher, Viking Penguin, a division of Penguin USA, and her agent, Sterling Lord Literistic, Inc. Thanks also to Bonnie Carlson.

We deeply appreciate the contributions of the following suppliers: Cam Steel Die Rule Works Inc. (steel cutting die for display); Canadian Pacific Forest Products Ltd. (text stock); ComCom (text typesetting); Horizon Paper Co., Inc. and Domtar Fine Papers (cover stock); MCUSA (display header); Delta Corrugated Container (corrugated display); Phototype Color Graphics (cover color separations); and Arcata Graphics Company/Buffalo (cover and text printing and binding).

Our thanks to Paul Davis Studio and Myrna Davis, Paul Davis, Jeanine Esposito, Alex Ginns and Frank Begrowicz for their inspired design of the covers of these books. Thanks also to Caron Harris for her sensitive design of the interior of this book; Karen Bernath for design of maps and diagrams; and Ron Bel Bruno for his timely help.

Contents

Oprah Winfrey played Mattie Michael
in the television movie *The Women of
Brewster Place*. (Photograph copyright
© Steve Fenn, Capital Cities/ABC, Inc.)

Note
To the Reader

The Women of Brewster Place is a novel about seven women who end up living in the same run-down, poor neighborhood: Brewster Place. Each chapter in the novel is about a different woman. The author, Gloria Naylor, reveals what brings each woman to Brewster Place. She describes how each woman tries to deal with her problems through strength and courage.

Every writer has a special voice. That is why we call our series *Writers' Voices*. We chose *The Women of Brewster Place* because Gloria Naylor's voice can be clearly heard as she tells us about these women's lives. In choosing a part from her book, we selected Mattie Michael's story. The selection tells about the period of her life that led her to Brewster Place.

Reading "About the Selection from *The Women of Brewster Place*," on page 12, will help you begin thinking about what you will read in the selection.

In addition to a selection from *The Women of Brewster Place*, this book includes chapters with interesting and helpful information related to the story. You may read these before or after reading the story. You may choose to read some or all of these chapters.

- If you would like more information about real people who, like the character Mattie, moved from the South to live and work in northern cities, look at the chapter called "About the Great Black Migration," on page 58.

- Many readers enjoy finding out about the person who wrote the story. Sometimes this information gives you more insight into the story. You can find out more about Gloria Naylor on page 54.

If you are a new reader, you may want to have this book read aloud to you, perhaps more than once. Even if you are a more experienced reader, you may enjoy hearing it read aloud before reading it silently to yourself.

We encourage you to read *actively*. Here are some things you can do.

BEFORE READING

- Read the front and back covers of the book, and look at the cover illustration. Ask yourself what you expect the book to be about.

- Think about why you want to read this book. Perhaps you have seen Oprah Winfrey's TV show *Brewster Place*. Perhaps you enjoy reading stories about characters who seem to have the same experiences as real people.

- Look at the Contents page. See where you can find a chronology of the events in the story and other information. Decide what you want to read and in what order.

DURING READING

- There may be words that are difficult to read. Keep reading to see if the meaning becomes clear. If it doesn't, go back and reread the difficult part or discuss it with others. Or look up the words in a dictionary.

- Ask yourself questions as you read. For example: Is it possible to love someone or something too much?

AFTER READING

- Think about what you have read. Did you identify with Mattie? Did the story make you see any of your own experiences in a new light?

- Talk with others about your thoughts.

- Try some of the questions and activities in "Questions for the Reader," on page 48. They are meant to help you discover more about what you have read and how it relates to you.

The editors of *Writers' Voices* hope you will write to us. We want to know your thoughts about our books.

About the Selection
from
The Women of Brewster Place

In *The Women of Brewster Place*, Gloria Naylor writes about the struggles of black women to live, love and survive in a big American city.

Brewster Place is an imaginary community in a northern city like Chicago or New York. Gloria Naylor created this community to represent all the black urban communities across America.

For Naylor, Brewster Place is the end of the line. It symbolizes hopelessness, poverty and broken dreams. When you have nowhere else to go, you end up in Brewster Place.

The selection tells the story of Mattie Michael and how she comes to live in

Brewster Place. In the beginning, Mattie and her baby son, Basil, come from the South to a northern city. After finding only dirty and rat-infested apartments, Mattie is ready to leave and go back home to the South.

On the way to the bus station, Mattie meets an old woman, Miss Eva. She lives in a big house in a nice neighborhood with her granddaughter, Lucielia. Miss Eva invites Mattie and Basil to live with her.

Nearly 18 years go by. Notice on pages 29–30 how Gloria Naylor describes this passage of time. She gives us a mental picture of Basil sitting on a chair. As time goes on, Basil's legs grow longer and extend past the different rungs on the chair. When his legs have grown past the bottom rung, we know that he has grown up and become a man. (You'll find a chronology of the events in the story on page 45.)

During this long period of time, Miss Eva dies and Mattie buys Miss Eva's house from her children. Late one night, Mattie receives a phone call that will change her life forever.

In the selection, we learn about Mattie's life and how she comes to end up in Brewster Place.

Naylor never tells us the exact years during which this story occurs. Perhaps she is telling us that the story is timeless. It could have taken place yesterday, or can happen today or tomorrow. Her point is that the problems of women like Mattie remain the same.

As you are reading, take note of how the author describes the times and places in the story. Perhaps you might think about how the place where a person lives affects his or her life.

Selected from
THE WOMEN OF BREWSTER PLACE
Gloria Naylor

1

One Friday night Mattie was asleep with
Basil, and he had squirmed out of her
arms and lay on his stomach near the
edge of the bed. His bottle had fallen out
of his mouth and rolled on the floor next
to the blanket. A rat crept out of the hole
behind the dresser and cautiously sniffed
around the wall for crumbs. Finding
nothing, it grew bolder in its search and
circled slowly toward the bed. It had
learned to fear the human smell but the
stillness of the bodies and its hunger drew
it nearer to the bed. It was about to turn
away and begin a new search toward the
wall when it smelled the dried milk and
sugar. Giving a squeak of anticipation, it
edged toward the smell and found the

baby's bottle. It licked the sweet crusted milk around the hole of the nipple and tried to gnaw through the thick rubber. Then the same smell drifted down from above its head, and, abandoning the nipple, it crawled up the blanket toward the fresh aroma of milk, sugar, and saliva. It licked around the baby's chin and lips, and when there was nothing left, it sought more and sank its fangs into the soft flesh.

"Oh, God!" she cried as she saw the blood dripping down his cheek from the two small punctures. She tried to calm the wailing child against her chest but he sensed her fear and continued to scream. She put him on the bed and cleaned his cheek with alcohol and rocked and soothed him down into a whimper. She reached for his bottle and, seeing the gnawed nipple, threw it against the wall in anger and disgust. The shattering glass frightened the child again, and he began to cry and Mattie cried with him.

She sat up all night with the lights on, and Basil finally fell into a fitful sleep. The next morning she took him to the hospital for a tetanus shot and ointment for his cheek. She returned to the boardinghouse, picked up her clothes, and with her baby in one arm and her suitcase in the other, she went looking for another place to live.

As the evening approached she cursed the aching feet that were beginning to fail her and she cursed her haste in leaving the only shelter they had, but then she thought about the gnawed bottle nipple and kept walking. She had her week's pay; she could go to a hotel. She could buy a one-way ticket home. Tomorrow was Sunday; she could look again. She could go home. If she found nothing Sunday, she could try again Monday. She could go home. If nothing Monday, she must show at work for Tuesday. Who would keep the baby? She could go home. Home. Home.

In her confusion Mattie had circled the same block twice. She remembered passing that old white woman just minutes before.

"Where you headin' with that pretty red baby? You lost, child?"

Mattie looked for the direction of the voice.

"If you wants the bus depot, you walkin' in the wrong direction, 'cause nobody in their right mind would be trying to walk to the train station. It's clear on the other side of town."

Mattie realized that the old woman was actually talking to her, but it was a black voice. She hesitantly approached the fence and stared incredulously into a pair of watery blue eyes.

"What you gapin' at? You simple-minded or something? I asked if you lost?"

Mattie saw that the evening light had hidden the yellow undertones in the finely wrinkled white face, and it had softened the broad contours of the woman's pug nose and full lips.

"Yes, mam. I mean, no, mam," she stammered. "I was looking for a place to stay and couldn't find none, so I was looking for the bus depot, I guess," she finished confusedly.

"What, you plan on sleeping in the depot with that baby tonight? . . . Well, where'd you sleep last night?" the woman said softly. "You get kicked out?"

"No, mam." And Mattie told her about the boardinghouse and the rat.

"And you just pick up and leave with no place to stay? Ain't that a caution. Whyn't you just plug up the hole with some steel wool and stay there till you could get better?"

Mattie tightened her arm around Basil and shook her head. There was no way she could have slept another night in that place without nightmares of things that would creep out of the walls to attack her child. She could never take him back to a place that had caused him so much pain.

The woman looked at the way she held the child and understood.

"Ya know, you can't keep him runnin' away from things that hurt him. Sometimes, you just gotta stay there and teach him how to go through the bad and good of whatever comes."

Mattie grew impatient with the woman. She didn't want a lecture about taking care of her son.

"If you'll just show me the way to the depot, I'll be obliged, mam," she said coldly. "Or if you know somewhere that has a room."

The woman chuckled. "No need to go gettin' snippy. That's one of the privileges of old age—you can give plenty of advice 'cause most folks think that's all you got left anyway. Now I may know of something available and I may not," she said, her eyes narrowing. "You workin'?"

Mattie told her where she worked.

"Where's your husband?"

Mattie knew this question was coming, and she was tempted to say that he had been killed in the war, but that would be a denial of her son, and she felt nothing shameful about what he was.

"I ain't got one." And she bent down and picked up her suitcase.

"Well," the old woman chuckled, "I've had five—outlived 'em all. So I can tell you, you ain't missing much." She opened the gate. "Since you done already picked up your valise, you might as well come on in and get that boy out the night air. Got plenty of room here. Just me and my grandbaby. He'll be good company for Lucielia."

Mattie followed her up the stone steps, trying to adjust her mind to this rapid turn of events and nameless old woman who had altered their destinies.

"Don't mind the house, child. I know it's a mess but I ain't got the strength I once had to keep it tidy. I guess you all must be hungry. Come on in the kitchen." And she headed for the back of the house with the baby.

Mattie was beginning to collect herself. "But I don't even know your name!" she called out, still fixed to the living room floor.

The old woman turned around. "That mean you can't eat my food? Well, since you gotta be properly introduced, the name of what's in the kitchen is pot roast, oven-browned potatoes, and string beans. And I believe there's even some angel food cake waitin' to make your acquaintance." She started toward the kitchen again and threw over her shoulder, "And the crazy old woman you're sure by now you're talkin' to is Eva Turner."

Mattie hurried behind Eva and Basil into the kitchen.

"I meant no offense, Mrs. Turner. It's just that this was all so quick and you've really been kind and my name is Mattie Michael and this is Basil and I don't even know how much space you got for us or how much you want to charge or anything, so you can see why I'm a little confused, can't you?" she finished helplessly.

The woman listened to her rattled introduction with calm amusement. "People 'round here call me Miss Eva." She put the baby on the polished tile floor and went to the stove. She seemed to ignore Mattie and hummed to herself while she heated and stirred the food.

Mattie was beginning to wonder if the woman might actually be a bit insane, and she looked around the kitchen for some sign of it. All she saw was rows of polished copper pots, huge potted plants, and more china bric-a-brac. There was a child's playpen pushed in the corner with piles of colorful rubber toys. Basil had seen the toys also and was tottering toward them. Mattie went to stop him, and he cried out in protest.

Miss Eva turned from the stove. "Leave him be. He ain't botherin' nothing. Them's Lucielia's toys, and she's asleep now."

"Who's Lucielia?" Mattie asked.

Miss Eva looked as if she were now doubting Mattie's sanity. "I told you outside—that's my son's child. I've had her since she was six months old. Her parents went back to Tennessee and just left the baby. Neither of 'em are worth the spit it takes to cuss 'em. But then, I can't blame her daddy none. He takes after his father—my last husband, who I shouldn't of never married, but I was always partial to dark-skinned men."

She brought the plates of food to the table, and while Mattie ate, Miss Eva insisted on feeding Basil. The young black woman and the old yellow woman sat in the kitchen for hours, blending their lives so that what lay behind one and ahead of the other became indistinguishable.

You like fried onions? I'll make us some liver and fried onions for Sunday supper tomorrow."

"That would be nice, mam, but you haven't told me yet what it'll cost to stay here with our room and board."

"I ain't runnin' no boardinghouse, girl; this is my home. But there's spare room upstairs that you're welcome to, along with the run of the house."

"But I can't stay without paying something," Mattie insisted, "and with you offering to mind the baby, too—I can't take advantage like that. Please, what will it cost?"

"All right," Miss Eva said, as she looked at the sleeping child in her arms, "I ain't decided yet, but in time I'll let you know."

Mattie was too sleepy to argue any further; she could hardly keep her eyes open. Miss Eva showed her to the bedroom upstairs, and Mattie was to die with the memory of the smell of lemon oil and the touch of cool, starched linen on her first night—of the thirty years of nights—she would spend in that house.

2

Mattie got up Sunday morning to the usual banging and howling in the house on weekends. Miss Eva was in the kitchen fighting with the children.

Mattie stood yawning in the kitchen door. "Can't there be just one morning of peace and quiet in this house—just one?" Ciel and Basil both ran to her, each trying to outshout the other about their various injustices. "I don't want to hear it," Mattie sighed. "It's too early for this nonsense. Now go wash up for breakfast—you're still in pajamas."

"Didn't you hear her? Now, get!" Miss Eva shouted and raised her spoon.

The children ran upstairs. Eva smiled

behind their backs and turned toward the stove.

"Well, good morning," Mattie said, and poured herself a cup of coffee.

" 'Tain't natural, just 'tain't natural," Miss Eva grumbled at the stove.

"They're only children, Miss Eva. All children are like that."

"I ain't talking about them children, I'm talking 'bout you. You done spent another weekend holed up in this house and ain't gone out nowhere."

"What I'm talkin' 'bout is that I ain't heard you mention no man involved in all them exciting goings-on in your life—church and children and work. It ain't natural for a young woman like you to live that way. I can't remember the last time no man come by to take you out."

"Humph." Mattie shrugged her shoulders and sipped her coffee. "I've been so busy, I guess I haven't noticed. It has been a long time, but so what? I've got my hands full raising my son."

"No young woman wants an empty bed, year in and year out."

"My bed hasn't been empty since Basil

was born," she said lightly, "and I don't think anyone but me would put up with the way that boy kicks in his sleep."

"Basil needs a bed of his own. I been telling you that for years."

"He's afraid of the dark. You know that."

"Five years old ain't no baby," Miss Eva said. And then she added mildly, "You sure it's Basil who don't want to sleep alone?"

"I don't have to take this," Mattie stammered defensively. "Just because we stay in your house don't give you a right to tell me how to raise my child. I'm a boarder here, or at least I would be if you'd let me pay you. Just tell me how much I owe you, and I'll pay up and be out before the week's over."

"I ain't decided yet."

"You been saying that for five years!" Mattie was frustrated.

"And you been movin' every time I mention anything about that little spoiled nigger of yours. You still saving my rent money in the bank, ain't you?"

"Of course." Mattie had religiously put

aside money every month, and her account had grown quite large.

"Good, you'll be using it soon enough for new clothes for my funeral. That is, if you plan on coming?"

"You're a crafty old woman. You always try to win an argument by talkin' about some funeral. You're too ornery to die, and you know it."

Miss Eva chuckled. "Some folks do say that. To tell you the truth, I had planned on stayin' till I'm a hundred."

Please do, Mattie thought sadly, and then said aloud, "No, I couldn't bear you that long—maybe till ninety-nine and a half."

They smiled at each other and silently agreed to put the argument to rest.

The children came running into the kitchen, scrubbed and penitent. "Let me check those ears," Mattie said to Ciel and Basil.

She was about to send him back upstairs to wash his when he put his arms around her neck and said, "Mama, I forgot to kiss you hello this morning." Basil knew he would win his reprieve this way. Miss Eva knew it, too, but she said nothing as she slung the oatmeal into their bowls and slowly shook her head.

Mattie was aware of only the joy that these unsolicited acts of tenderness gave her. She watched him eating his oatmeal, intent on each mouthful that he swallowed because it was keeping her son alive. It was moving through his blood and creating skin cells and hair cells and new muscles that would eventually uncurl and multiply and stretch the skin on his upper arms and thighs, elongate the plump legs that only reached the top rung of his chair. And when they had reached the second rung, Miss Eva would be dead. Her children would have descended upon the beautiful house and stripped it of all that was valuable and sold the rest to Mattie. Her parents would have carried away a screaming Ciel, and as Mattie would look around the gutted house, she'd know why the old yellow woman had made her save her money. She had wanted her spirit to remain in this house through the memory of someone who was capable of loving it as she had. While Basil's legs pushed down toward the third rung, Mattie would be working two jobs to carry the mortgage on the house. Her son must have room to grow in, a yard to run in, a decent place to bring his friends. Her own spirit must one day have a place to rest because the body could not, as it pushed and struggled to make all around them safe and comfortable. It would all be for him and those to come from the long, muscular thighs of him who sat opposite her at the table.

Mattie looked at the man who was gulping coffee and shoveling oatmeal into his mouth. "Why you eating so fast? You'll choke."

"I got some place to go."

"It's Sunday, Basil. You been runnin' all weekend. I thought you were gonna stay home and help me with the yard."

"Look, I'm only going out for a few minutes. I told you I'll cut the grass, and I will, so stop hassling me."

Mattie had never met any of Basil's girlfriends, and he rarely mentioned them. She thought about this as she gave him the money and watched him leave the house. She cleared off the breakfast dishes, and it suddenly came to her that she hadn't met many of his male friends, either. Where was he going? She truly didn't know, and it had come to be understood that she was not to ask. How long had it been that way? Surely it had happened within moments. It seemed that only hours ago he had been the child who could hug her neck and talk himself out of a spanking, who had brought home crayoned valentines, and had cried when she went to her second job. So then, who was this stranger who had done away with her little boy and left her with no one and so alone?

Mattie sat there for hours, and still Basil did not come. She looked through the windows at the long grass and decided to cut it the next day after work, if her back didn't bother her too much. It was becoming more difficult each year to keep up the house alone. She got up from the couch stiffly and climbed the steps toward her bedroom.

3

Mattie woke up trembling and lay dazed among the tangled bedcovers. She covered her ears to block out the shrill screams that continued to echo through her head. After a moment she realized that the noise was coming from the telephone on her nightstand. Her heart was still pounding as she blindly groped for the phone.

"Yes?"

"Mama, it's me."

She held the hard plastic receiver to her ear and tried to make sense out of the electrical impulses that were forming words—strange words that could have no possible association with the voice on the other end.

A bar. A woman. A fight. A booking.

"Basil?" Surely this voice was Basil's.

Fingerprints. Manslaughter. Lawyer.

Mattie sat up in bed, gripped the receiver, and tried to follow these new words as they came flying out of the receiver and spun bizarre patterns in her head. She was frantically trying to link them into sentences, phrases—anything that she could place within her world—but it all made no sense.

"What are you talking about?" she yelled into the phone.

". . . And the son-of-a-bitches beat me up! They beat me up, Mama!" And the voice began to cry.

This she understood. Conditioned by years of instinctual response to his tears, Mattie's head cleared immediately, and she jumped out of bed.

"Who beat you up? Where are you?"

"Baby, there ain't nothing to worry about," she told Basil as she stroked his hand, trying to calm the frightened look in his eyes. "I went to Reverend Kelly, and he referred me to a good criminal lawyer. Now he said it would be all right, and it will."

"When am I getting out of here? That's what I want to know." And he snatched his hand away and nervously drummed it on the table.

"Tomorrow, after some kind of hearing, they'll tell us when you'll go to trial."

"I don't understand this!" he exploded. "Why should there be a trial? It was an accident! And that guy was picking on me over some broad. I don't even know his name."

"I know, honey, but a man is dead, and there's gotta be some kind of proceeding about it."

"Well, he's better off than me. This place is a hellhole, and see what those bastards did to my face."

Mattie winced as she forced herself to stare at his bruised face. "They said you resisted arrest, Basil, and broke a policeman's wrist," she said softly.

"So what!" He glared at her. "They wanted to put me in jail for something that wasn't my fault. They had no right to do this to me, and now you're sticking up for them."

"Oh, Basil," Mattie sighed, suddenly feeling the strain of the last twelve hours, "I ain't sticking up for nobody, but we gotta face what happened so we can see our way clear from this."

"It's not 'we,' Mama, it's me. I'm stuck in here—not you. It's filthy and smelly, and I even heard rats under my bed last night."

Mattie's stomach knotted into tiny spasms.

"So when am I leaving?"

"Tomorrow at the hearing, when they tell us the bail, I'll put it up and then you can get out."

"Can't you give them the bail money today? I can't spend another night in this place."

"Basil, there's nothing I can do today. We have to wait." Mattie pressed a trembling hand to her eyes to hold back the tears. She had never felt so impotent in her life. There was no way she could fight the tiny inked markings that now controlled their lives. She would give anything to remove him from this horrible place—didn't he know that? But those blue loops, commas, and periods had tied her hands.

"Okay, fine. If you can't, you can't," he said bitterly, and got up from his chair.

"Honey, we still got time, don't you want to sit and talk?"

"There's nothing left to talk about, Mama, unless you wanna hear about the broken toilets with three-day-old shit or the bedbugs that have ate up my back or the greasy food I keep throwing up. Other than that, I got nothing to say to you."

He left Mattie sitting there, understanding his frustration but wishing he had chosen a kinder way of hurting her, by just hitting her in the face.

The judge set bail the next day, and Basil was given an early trial date. Cecil Garvin [Basil's lawyer] tried to appeal the bail, but the court denied his plea.

"I'm sorry, Mrs. Michael, it's the best I could do. There's no need, really, to try and raise so much money. The case goes to trial in only two weeks, and it won't be a complicated proceeding. I've talked to the district attorney, and they won't push too heavily on the assault charge if we drop the implications of undue force in the arrest. So it's going to work out well for all the parties involved. And your son will be free in less than fifteen days."

"I still want to put up the bail," Mattie said.

Garvin looked worried. "It's a great deal of money, Mrs. Michael, and you don't have the ready assets for something like that."

"I've got my house; it's mine and paid for. Can't I put that up for bail?"

"Well, yes, but you do understand that bail is only posted to insure that the defendant appears for trial. If they don't appear, the court issues a bench warrant for the truant party and you forfeit your bond. You do understand that?"

"I understand."

The snow fell early that year. When Basil and Mattie left the precinct, the wide soft flakes were floating in gentle layers on the November air. Basil reached out and tried to grab one to give her, and he laughed as it melted in his hand.

"Remember how I used to cry when I tried to bring you a snowflake and it always disappeared?" He held his face up to the sky and let the snow fall on his closed lids. "Oh, God, Mama, isn't it beautiful?"

"Beautiful? You always hated the snow."

"Not now, it's wonderful. It's out here and free, like I am. I love it!" And he wrapped his arms around himself.

Mattie's insides expanded to take in his joy.

"And I love you, Mama." He put his arm around her shoulder and squeezed. "Thank you."

The lawyer called at the end of the second week to remind them of the court appointment, and Basil grew irritable. He told her he hated the thought of that place. He had tried to pretend that it didn't exist, and he had been so happy. Now this. What if something went wrong and they kept him again? You couldn't trust those honky lawyers—what did they care about him? Those people in that bar weren't friends of his—what if they changed their stories? What if the girl hated him now and decided to lie? He remembered the way she had screamed over the dead man's body. Yes, she would lie to get back at him. He knew it.

"I'll blow my brains out before I spend my life in jail," he said to Mattie while driving her to work.

"Basil, stop talkin' stupidness!" Her voice was sharp. She had not been able to sleep well the last two nights, lying and listening to him pacing around in his room. "I've been hearing nothing but nonsense the last coupla days, and I'm sick of it."

"Nonsense!" He swung his head around.

"Yes, damned nonsense! You ain't going to jail 'cause you ain't done nothing to go to jail for. We go to court Tuesday; they'll give all the evidence, and you'll be clear. That's all there is to it. The lawyer said so, and he should know."

"Mama, he'll say anything to get your

money. If someone offered him a nickel more than you paid, he'd throw me in jail personally and swallow the key. You don't know them like I do, and you don't know what it's like in those cells. And they'll send me to a worse place than some county jail." He looked at her sorrowfully. "I couldn't stand it, Mama. I just couldn't."

She felt him looking at her turned head from time to time and knew he was puzzled by her silence. He was waiting to be coaxed and petted into a lighter mood, but she forced herself to keep staring out the window. When the car pulled up to her job, she mumbled a good-bye and reached for the latch. Basil grabbed her hand, leaned over, and kissed her cheek.

"Good-bye, Mama."

She was touched by the gentleness in his caress and immediately repentant of her attitude in the car. During the day she resolved to make amends to him. After all, he was under a great deal of pressure, and it wasn't fair that he bear it alone. Was it so wrong that he seemed to need her constant support? Had he not been trained to expect it? And he had been trying so hard those last two weeks; she couldn't let him down now. She would go home and make him a special dinner— creamed chicken with rice—he always loved that. Then they would sit and talk, and she would tell him, once again, or as many times as needed, that it was going to be all right.

Basil wasn't waiting for Mattie when she finished work, so she took the bus home and stopped by the store to pick up the things she needed for his dinner. She walked up the street and saw that his car wasn't parked out front and the house was dark. She stood for a moment by the front gate, first looking at the space where the car should be and then at the unlit windows. Normally she would have gone through the front door, taken off her coat, and hung it in the front hall closet. Tonight she entered the house through the back door that led straight into the kitchen. She took off her coat and laid it on one of the kitchen chairs. There was an extra jacket of his in the front hall closet that would not be there.

She washed her hands at the sink and immediately started to cut up the chicken and peel and slice vegetables. Her feet were beginning to ache, but her house slippers were in the living room, under a table where his portable radio would not be, so she limped around her kitchen while finishing his dinner. She let the water run in the sink longer than necessary and dropped her knife and set the pots on the stove with a fraction of extra force. She made as much noise as she could to ward off the stillness of the upstairs bedroom that kept trying to creep into her kitchen, carrying empty drawers and closets, a vacant space where a suitcase had lain, missing toothpaste. She banged pot lids and beat sauces in aluminum bowls until her arms were tired. She watched and fussed over his dinner, opening and closing the oven door a dozen times—anything to keep back the stillness until he would drive up in his car, say he had come to his senses, sit down and eat her creamed chicken, save a lifetime of work lying in the bricks of her home.

The vegetables were done, the chicken almost burnt, and the biscuits had to come out of the oven. She turned off the gas jets, opened the oven door, and banged the pan of biscuits onto the countertop. She looked frantically at the creeping shadows over her kitchen door and rushed to the cabinet and took out plates and silverware. She slammed the cabinet shut and slowly and noisily set the table for two. She looked pleadingly around the kitchen, but there was nothing left to be done. So she pulled out the kitchen chair, letting the metal legs drag across the tiles. Trembling, she sat down, put her head in her hands, and waited for the patient and crouching stillness just beyond the kitchen door.

A hand touched her shoulder, and Mattie gave a small cry.

"Didn't mean to startle you, mam, but it's snowing pretty bad, and we gotta move this stuff upstairs. Would you please go up and unlock the door?"

At first Mattie looked vacantly into the face of the man, and then her mind snapped into place from its long stretch over time. The cab had just backed out of Brewster Place, and she watched it turn down the avenue and drive away. Her eyes trailed slowly along the cracked stoops and snow-filled gutters until they came to her building. She glanced at the wall and, with an inner sigh, remembered her plants again.

The mover who had addressed her was staring at her uncomfortably.

"Oh, yes, I'm sorry," she said disconcertedly. "I have the keys right here, don't I?" And she opened her pocketbook and started searching for them.

The two men looked at each other, and one shrugged his shoulders and pointed his finger toward his head.

Mattie grasped the cold metal key in one hand and put the other on the iron railing and climbed the stoop to the front entrance. As she opened the door and entered the dingy hallway, a snowflake caught in her collar, melted, and rolled down her back like a frozen tear.

A Chronology of Events
In the Selection

Before the Selection Begins: Mattie
Michael and her baby Basil move from
the South to a northern city. They stay
in a boardinghouse.

When Basil Is a Baby
Basil is bitten by a rat, page 16.
Mattie looks for a new place to live,
page 17.
Mattie and Basil meet Miss Eva, pages
17–19.
Mattie and Basil move in with Miss Eva
and her granddaughter Lucielia,
pages 20–24.

About Five Years Later: Miss Eva and
Mattie talk in the kitchen. Miss Eva

tells Mattie to stop babying Basil. Pages 26–28.

Time Passes: Miss Eva dies and Mattie buys the house, page 29.

More Time Passes (About 20 Years): Basil grows up. Mattie is much older. Basil eats breakfast and goes out. Page 30.

That Night: Basil gets in a fight. The other man dies. Basil is arrested. He calls Mattie from jail. Pages 32–33.

The Next Day: Mattie visits Basil in jail. He begs her to get him out. Pages 33–36.

The Next Day: Basil has a hearing and the judge sets bail. The lawyer, Cecil Garvin, explains bail to Mattie. Bail is money held by the court. When bail is posted, the defendant can leave jail while he or she is awaiting trial. If the defendant does not show up for the court trial, the money is forfeited. The lawyer thinks Mattie should not put up bail for Basil. The bail is a lot of money and Basil only needs to stay in jail for two weeks before his trial. But Mattie wants Basil to be free. She decides to put up her house for Basil's bail. Pages 36–37.

Soon After: Basil and Mattie drive home from jail, pages 37–38.

One Week Later: Basil's trial is in one week. He is worried that he will have to go back to jail. Basil drives Mattie to work. Pages 39–40.

That Evening
   Basil doesn't meet Mattie when she gets off work, page 41.
   Mattie goes home to wait for Basil. She cooks his favorite dinner. Pages 41–42.
   Basil doesn't come back. Since Mattie put up her house for bail, she has lost the house. She has also lost Basil. Page 43.

A Few Weeks Later: Mattie has to leave her house and move to Brewster Place, pages 43–44.

Questions
For the Reader

THINKING ABOUT THE STORY

1. What was interesting for you about the selection from *The Women of Brewster Place*?

2. Were there ways the events or people in the selection became important or special to you? Write about or discuss these.

3. What do you think were the most important things Gloria Naylor wanted to say in the selection?

4. In what ways did the selection answer the questions you had before you began reading or listening?

5. Were any parts of the selection difficult to understand? If so, you may want to read or listen to them again. Discuss with your learning partners possible reasons why they were difficult.

THINKING ABOUT THE WRITING

1. How did Gloria Naylor help you see, hear and feel what happened in the selection? Find the words, phrases or sentences that did this best.

2. Writers think carefully about their stories' settings, characters and events. When writing this selection, which of these things do you think Gloria Naylor felt was most important? Find the parts of the story that support your opinion.

3. In the selection, Gloria Naylor uses dialogue. Dialogue can make a story more alive. Pick out some dialogue that you feel is strong, and explain how it helps the story.

4. The selection from *The Women of*

Brewster Place is written from the point of view of someone outside the story who tells us what is happening. The writer uses the words "he" and "she" rather than "I" or "me." What difference does this create in the writing of the selection?

5. Gloria Naylor, through her writing, makes us understand the strength of Mattie's love for Basil. Find some parts in the selection that helped you understand how much she loved and protected Basil.

ACTIVITIES

1. Were there any words that were difficult for you in the selection from *The Women of Brewster Place*? Go back to these words and try to figure out their meanings. Discuss what you think each word means, and why you made that guess. Look them up in a dictionary and see if your definitions are the same or different.

Discuss with your learning partners how you are going to remember each word. Some ways to remember words are to put them on file cards, to write them in a journal or to create a personal dictionary. Be sure to use the words in your writing in a way that will help you to remember their meanings.

2. Talking with other people about what you have read can increase your understanding. Discussion can help you to organize your thoughts, get new ideas and to rethink your original ideas. Discuss your thoughts about the selection with someone else who has read it. Find out if you helped yourself understand the selection in the same or different ways. Find out if your opinions about the selection are the same or different. See if your thoughts change as a result of this discussion.

3. After you finish reading or listening, you might want to write down your thoughts about the book. You could write your reflections on the book in a journal, or you could write about topics the book

has brought up that you want to explore further. You could write a book review or a letter to a friend you think might be interested in the book.

4. Did reading the selection give you any ideas for your own writing? You might want to write about:

- your own relationship with your father, mother, son or daughter,

- how the place you live in affects your life,

- what you would do if you lost everything.

5. Why does a person move from one place to another? You might want to interview some of your friends and find out how they came to live where they do. Where did they live before? Did moving change their lives for the better or for the worse? Did they want to move? You might want to compare their stories with your own.

6. If you could talk to Gloria Naylor, what questions would you ask about her writing? You might want to write the questions in a journal.

About Gloria Naylor

Gloria Naylor knows what it's like to live in a big city. She was born in New York City in 1950. She grew up there and still lives there today. She always wanted to be a writer.

In an interview in the *Southern Review*, she said, "From grade school I had been told that I had potential, while I only knew that I felt most comfortable when expressing myself through the written word. So I scribbled on bits of looseleaf and in diaries to hide it all away."

After graduating from high school in 1968, Naylor attended Brooklyn College and studied English. She also worked as a nurse and later got her master's degree in Afro-American Studies from Yale University.

Gloria Naylor says that one of her biggest influences was another black woman writer, Toni Morrison. Morrison's books include *The Song of Solomon* and *Beloved*. Knowing that another black woman was successfully expressing her feelings through writing gave Naylor the inspiration that she needed to begin to write for a living.

The Women of Brewster Place was published in 1980. It is Naylor's first novel. She chose to write about women because, she says, "As far as men are concerned, women have no history because they do not really exist." In *The Women of Brewster Place*, she calls attention to that very history.

Ms. Naylor received the American Book Award for this novel. It was also turned into a movie and television series starring Oprah Winfrey.

Naylor has written two other books, *Linden Hills* and *Mama Day*.

MAP OF THE GREAT BLACK MIGRATION

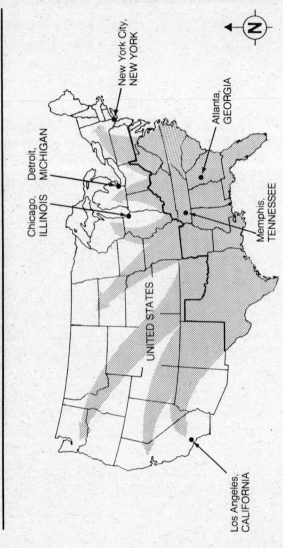

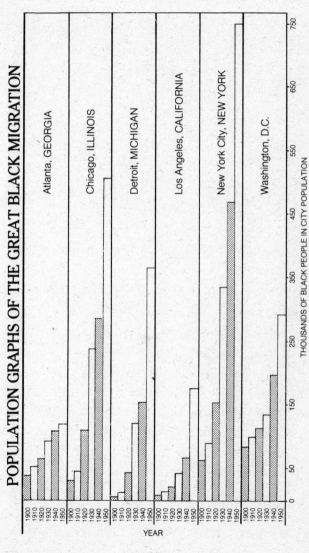

POPULATION GRAPHS OF THE GREAT BLACK MIGRATION

Atlanta, GEORGIA

Chicago, ILLINOIS

Detroit, MICHIGAN

Los Angeles, CALIFORNIA

New York City, NEW YORK

Washington, D.C.

THOUSANDS OF BLACK PEOPLE IN CITY POPULATION

YEAR

About the
Great Black Migration

In the beginning of this century, 90 percent of the black population of the United States lived in the South. By 1950, only 63 percent remained there. By 1970, nearly half of the blacks lived in the North. What made southern blacks move north and west?

In the early 1900s, most southern blacks did not own their land but worked as low-paid farm laborers. The South was home to "Jim Crow" laws that forced blacks to use separate public facilities such as restrooms, schools and even drinking fountains. Black schools were inferior to white schools and most black children never got a chance at a good education. Violence against blacks was common in the South.

It wasn't until World War I that things began to change. Many men went to fight the war overseas, and northern employers who had not hired blacks before began to do so. The word spread quickly through the South.

From 1910 to 1920, some 470,000 black Southerners left their homes and ventured north. The North, it was said, was the promised land that did not have discrimination and where fair wages were paid. Black-owned newspapers urged their readers, "Go North, where there is more humanity, some justice and fairness."

Many packed up their entire families and boarded trains, spending their life's savings on the trip. Some sent ahead only one member of the family to pave the way for the rest. Often, single parents made the trip with their children. Others moved north one step at a time, first settling in large southern cities such as Atlanta or Memphis.

This pattern continued for the next 50

years and changed the very makeup of our country. During World War II, 330,000 blacks left the South and joined the already overflowing populations of northern cities.

The North was not the dream blacks had hoped for. Although the Ford Motor Company in Detroit, Michigan, promised wages of five dollars a day, the cost of living was much higher there than it was in the South. In 1943, Detroit witnessed a racial riot. The population increases of the city had left little available housing and few new jobs. Tensions between blacks and whites finally exploded, leaving 34 people dead.

Housing discrimination in the North forced blacks into the outskirts of cities where the apartments were old and often very costly. Whole families would crowd into one-room apartments without running water or heat. Overcrowding left many without a home at all. The Chicago Urban League reported that in one day, 664 blacks applied for a meager 50 housing units. Even in 1960, 40 percent of all black-occupied housing lacked adequate plumbing facilities.

White communities prevented blacks from moving within their boundaries, confining the blacks to small poverty-stricken areas. It wasn't until 1968 that the Federal Fair Housing Law was passed in order to end such practices.

From 1950 to 1960, a record number of 1,457,000 black Southerners moved north, a large number of them women. They experienced not only discrimination as blacks but also as women. They were confined to such jobs as waitresses and housekeepers, working 12 hours or more a day. Domestic workers often had to live with their employers, seeing their own families only on Sundays.

Yet living in the North did have its advantages. Because children did not have to help with farmwork, they could get an education. The schools they attended were better and some of the students went on to college. By the 1940s, blacks in the North were more easily accepted into professions such as medicine, law and education. The children of the first black immigrants grew up to find better jobs, higher wages and improved living conditions.

SUGGESTED READING:
OTHER BOOKS
BY BLACK WOMEN AUTHORS

ZORA NEALE HURSTON
Their Eyes Were Watching God
University of Illinois Press
Urbana and Chicago 1978

ANNE MOODY
Coming of Age in Mississippi
Dell Publishing Co.
New York 1976

TONI MORRISON
Beloved
Alfred A. Knopf, Inc.
New York 1987

SOJOURNER TRUTH
Narrative of Sojourner Truth
Arno Press & The New York Times
New York 1968

ALICE WALKER
The Color Purple
Harcourt Brace Jovanovich
San Diego 1982

Seven series of good books for all readers:

WRITERS' VOICES
Selections from the works of America's finest and most popular writers, along with background information, maps, and other supplementary materials. Authors include: Kareem Abdul-Jabbar • Maya Angelou • Bill Cosby • Alex Haley • Stephen King • Loretta Lynn • Larry McMurtry • Amy Tan • Anne Tyler • Abigail Van Buren • Alice Walker • Tom Wolfe, and many others.

NEW WRITERS' VOICES
Anthologies and individual narratives by adult learners. A wide range of topics includes home and family, prison life, and meeting challenges. Many titles contain photographs or illustrations.

OURWORLD
Selections from the works of well-known science writers, along with related articles and illustrations. Authors include David Attenborough and Carl Sagan.

FOR YOUR INFORMATION
Clearly written and illustrated works on important self-help topics. Subjects include: Eating Right • Managing Stress • Getting Fit • About AIDS • Getting Good Health Care, among others.

TIMELESS TALES
Classic myths, legends, folk tales, and other stories from around the world, with special illustrations.

SPORTS
Fact-filled books on baseball, football, basketball, and boxing, with lots of action photos. With read-along tapes narrated by Phil Rizzuto, Frank Gifford, Dick Vitale, and Sean O'Grady.

SULLY GOMEZ MYSTERIES
Fast-paced detective series starring Sully Gomez and the streets of Los Angeles.

WRITE FOR OUR FREE COMPLETE CATALOG:

SIGNAL HILL

Signal Hill Publications
P.O. Box 131
Syracuse, NY 13210-0131